TABLE OF CONTENT

INTRODUCTION

Life is amazing, isn't it? It's this magical whirlwind of learning, fun, adventure, growth, and discovery. Each day brings with it something new and unique which is pretty incredible, don't you think?

Empowering
STORIES FOR
AMAZING GIRLS

MOTIVATIONAL BOOK FOR KIDS TO INSPIRE CONFIDENCE,
SELF-LOVE AND FRIENDSHIP AMONG CHILDREN

Sophie Potter

ISBN: 979-8-9865737-1-7

Copyright 2023 ©

Authored by Sophie Potter

Disclaimer.

All rights reserved.

There are so many opportunities in life to do things that make you happy, excited, grateful, and inspired. These are the things that make us skip with joy and feel giddy with excitement. There are so many new things for us to try, explore, and feel delighted about.

But as incredible as life can be, at times, it can also be rather confusing. Sometimes your emotions might take over and leave you feeling sad, angry, disappointed, or afraid.

It's normal to feel a mixture of emotions about certain situations. It's by taking a deep breath and trying our best to understand these feelings and embracing them that we're able to move forward.

Everyone reacts in the wrong way sometimes and makes bad decisions. But everyone also reacts in the right way sometimes and makes amazing decisions. We don't always make the right call but by learning from the bad we're able to grow into the good.

It's okay to be unsure of things and to question your feelings and emotions. Feeling this way is a normal part of being human. Sometimes deciding what you should do may seem daunting but you're not alone in feeling like this.

In this book, you'll meet seven amazing girls who all face a different set of challenges.

And there's Jasmine, who on learning a new skill finds herself doubting her own abilities. When an emergency situation happens will she be able to find her inner strength and step up to the task?

Cassie is wary of the old lady in the park because she doesn't act or dress the same way as she does. Will an unexpected event lead Cassie to look beyond someone's appearance and see the true person beneath?

There's a new girl at Ava's school and some of the other children aren't being very nice to her. Will Ava be able to show kindness and support to this girl and help her find the confidence to shine?

Eloise worries that having braces fitted will lead to her friends thinking she's uncool and teasing her. Will she be able to put her worries aside and accept this change in her appearance?

Amelia is terrified of talking to strangers but she knows that she's going to have to do it if she wants her favorite soccer ball back. Can she find the inner courage to overcome her fear?

Olivia is convinced that the lead role in the school play will be hers. So, when things don't go to plan can she find a way to look past her disappointment and embrace the opportunity she has been given?

After a nasty fall during a competition, Kimberley isn't sure if she wants to compete in gymnastics anymore. Will she find a way to overcome her fears and not give up on the sport she loves?

These girls don't always make the right decisions, and sometimes they find certain situations tricky. But just like you, they are kind, thoughtful, caring girls who always try to do what's best.

By allowing yourself to move forward in life, you're opening yourself up to discovering new hobbies, friends, and adventures. Who knows what amazing things this could lead you to?

There's so much to do and see in this world, so don't let a few obstacles stop you from doing so. It's best to find a way to overcome the hurdles that are in your way instead of just giving up on something that could end up being spectacular.

Don't dwell on past mistakes when instead, you could learn from them and go on to have exciting new adventures and experiences. You can't change the past but you can learn from it and embrace the future.

Always let your determination dazzle, your thoughtfulness twinkle, your bravery shine brightly, and your gentle nature glisten.

JASMINE'S NO TALK, ALL ACTION DAY

D o you ever dream about being a real-life superhero with a shiny cape who always swoops in at exactly the right moment to save the day?

Being around to prevent a crisis sounds great and all but it also sounds rather scary.

Normal life doesn't usually require you to zoom around at lightning speed and rescue fluffy kittens from burning buildings—but you might find yourself in a situation where a new skill might come in useful.

You may worry that your newly learned skill might disappear from your mind exactly at the moment in time when you need to use it.

Or that under pressure you'll be too flustered and frenzied to carry it out to the best of your ability.

It's normal to sometimes feel a little overwhelmed with new information and new skills.

Don't let your doubts and disbelief ever stop you from being your best superhero self, as with or without the shiny cape, you are an amazing girl.

It was the end of the junior scouts group meeting, and Jasmine was standing with her friends in the room. Today's meeting had been focused around completing the relevant tasks needed to earn their first-aid badge.

Jasmine stared down at her green vest where several badges were sewn on. Among her favorites were the cooking badge, where she'd made a delicious forest-themed cake with chocolate frosting; and a drawing badge, where she'd created a portfolio packed full of sketches of her beloved dog Buster.

She brushed her fingers over the spare spot where her first-aid badge would go, then let out a deflated sigh. Unlike cooking and drawing she found the tasks for the first-aid badge a lot harder to absorb. She knew that if she messed up first-aid then she could end up doing more harm than good, and this thought made her tummy feel like worms were wriggling in it.

"That was easy, right?" Emily said, her words breaking Jasmine from her thoughts. "I learned sooo much today. The next time someone from my family's sick I'll be able to nurse them back to health in no time."

"Yep, it was the easiest thing ever! I'm going to make up my very own first-aid box and carry it with me everywhere," Freya said confidently.

"Me too. I can see if mom will let me use her old sewing tub for it," Emily gave an affirming nod. "Jasmine, which first-aid emergency do you think you'll be best at?"

Jasmine gulped back in nerves and then fiddled with her vest. She didn't feel confident in anything she'd learned today—different snippets of information swirled around her head in a jumbled mess and she wasn't sure that if needed, she'd ever be able to unscramble them.

"I… um… I suppose I could treat a wound," she flustered out.

"You don't sound very sure," Emily giggled. "I hope I'm never in trouble when you're around."

"Me neither. I'd want to be around someone brave who isn't afraid of a little blood," Freya snorted.

"I'm not afraid of blood," Jasmine protested in a meek voice. "I just. I um, I just don't-" she trailed off her words and then sighed quietly to herself.

They'd completed all of the steps to earn their first-aid badge and the award ceremony would happen at the next meeting. As much as Jasmine longed to sew this badge on her vest, she felt undeserving of it. Her friends seemed so confident about what to do in a crisis while she was left feeling like a fraud.

…

On the walk home through the park, Jasmine messaged her mom telling her she was on her way. She was hoping she'd be left to do this walk alone but Emily and Freya tagged along too.

"I know how to put someone in a recovery position, do you want me to demonstrate to you?" Freya looked at Jasmine.

"Um no thanks," Jasmine forced a smile through her head shake.

"Oh, okay. I just thought it might be helpful, that's all. You don't want to earn your first-aid badge when you don't really know what you're doing."

"I do know what I'm doing," Jasmine muttered.

"What about a graze or cut—would you be able to handle the blood?" Emily asked.

"Uhm… I think so," she chewed on the side of her lip in doubt.

Both Emily and Freya exchanged knowing looks and then laughed.

Jasmine dipped her head and stared glumly down at her shoes. She walked a step ahead of her friends so she didn't have to talk to them anymore. It was a beautiful sunny day but she seemed unable to shake the fog from her mind.

She walked past an older boy sitting on a bench. Then she side-stepped out of the way as a little boy on a scooter who zoomed toward her and took a hand off the handlebar to wave at the older boy.

"Cole, pay attention and keep both hands on the handlebars," the older boy told him.

As Jasmine continued up the path, she tried to replay the different steps in her mind of how to treat a cut, when suddenly an echoing scream filled the air "AGGGHHH".

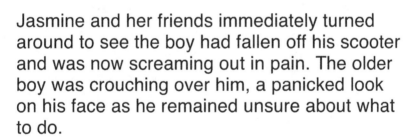

Jasmine and her friends immediately turned around to see the boy had fallen off his scooter and was now screaming out in pain. The older boy was crouching over him, a panicked look on his face as he remained unsure about what to do.

As scary as this was Jasmine sprung into action.

"Are you coming?" she asked her bewildered-looking friends.

Knowing that the little boy needed her help, she tried her best to remain calm and hurried over to him, her two friends slowly trailing behind her.

Firstly, she checked around to make sure the situation seemed safe for her to intervene, then she smiled at the older boy.

"Hi, I'm part of a girl scouts' group and today I finished my first-aid training," she said in a calm voice to reassure him. "Please can you tell me what happened?"

"It's my…my little brother, Cole. I told him not to go so fast. He…his head…his leg. He can't move his leg," the older boy stammered.

She could see that as well as having a nasty-looking cut on his head, the little boy's leg was red and swollen.

Knowing that the next step was calling for help, she passed the older boy her phone.

"Call an ambulance, that's a bad cut to his head so he might have a concussion, and I think his leg might be broken. Tell them to come to the path not far from the main entrance in Greenville Park. Then call your parents and tell them where you are and what happened."

Kneeling by the little boy she saw that he was sobbing as he peered down at his injured leg.

"Hi Cole, my name's Jasmine, I'm here to help. Can you show me where it hurts?"

The little boy pointed a shaking finger from his head to his leg and then he let out a fresh bout of tears.

"Cole, I think you're a really brave boy," she smiled at him. "I don't want you to do any more harm to your leg so do you think you can be even braver and keep it as still as you can for me?"

"Oh…um…o-okay," Cole sobbed out.

The wound on his head seemed to be bleeding, so she knew she needed to do something about that, only she didn't have anything on her. She turned and looked at her friends, who were lingering a few steps behind her, then asked them:

"Do either of you have a bandage or a tissue?"

Emily shook her head but Freya gave a timid nod, then searched around her pocket and held out a spare bandage she'd been given during their first-aid training.

"Awesome, thank you," she took it from her.

"Cole, I'm just going to wrap this around your head to try and stop the bleeding. Is that okay?" she said in a gentle voice.

The boy rubbed his wet eyes with his hands, sniffed back his sobs, and then gave a nod of agreement. She'd just finished wrapping the bandage when the older boy reappeared and knelt next to his brother.

"They're on their way, bud," he gave an awkward look at Cole.

"All done, I just need something to hold it in place. Ah, I know!" Jasmine pulled a pin out of her hair and used it to fasten the bandage, then she turned to the older brother. "Make sure the bandage stays on to stem the bleeding. Also keep him awake, as falling asleep with a concussion is dangerous."

She'd just finished talking to him when she spotted a frantic figure running toward them, followed by the paramedics.

"Mommy," the little boy cried.

"Don't worry, sweetie, mommy's here," she rushed to his side.

Jasmine stepped back and let the paramedics tend to Cole and then carefully fasten him onto a gurney.

"Well done young lady. Cole tells us you did a great job looking after him. You'd make an excellent paramedic one day," one of the paramedics said to her, as she wheeled Cole past her.

"Sweetie, thank you. Thank you so much," his mom gushed out.

"That's okay. I'm just glad I could help," Jasmine blushed.

"Yeah, um… thanks for everything. I panicked so I'm glad you were here," the older brother told her, as he walked past holding the scooter.

Jasmine watched them leave, then she peered around and realized something— her friends had gone. She carried on walking through the park when suddenly she spotted Emily and Freya sitting on the wall by the park entrance.

On seeing her approaching they jumped off the wall and hurried over to her.

"Is the little boy okay?" Freya asked.

18

"Yep, he's going to be fine. He's with his mom and the paramedics now."

"You were amazing—I wasn't. It's just so different when it's actually happening," Emily sighed. "I just froze and didn't know what to do. I'm um… I'm sorry for what I said before."

"Me too," Freya said coyly. "It's so much scarier when it's for real."

"That's okay. It was scary but seeing Cole hurt like that, I don't know, I just seemed to know exactly what I needed to do."

As Jasmine left the park with her friends, she realized she didn't feel useless or lacking in her own abilities anymore—instead, she stood up straight, with a proud smile on her face.

…

Next week at the scout's meeting, Jasmine beamed as she watched Clara, their group leader, call her friends up to the front to receive their first-aid badges.

Then when it was Jasmine's turn, Clara told the whole group about what'd happened in the park, then she pulled out a box of chocolates alongside the first-aid badge and handed them to her. Jasmine blushed with pride as the other scouts congratulated and applaud her.

As soon as the badge ceremony was over, Jasmine excitedly gripped her new badge and skipped over to her friends and offered them each a chocolate. As she popped a chocolate into her mouth she peered down at her badge with pride—she didn't doubt herself anymore and she knew she deserved this badge. She couldn't wait to go home and sew it onto her vest.

Most importantly of all, Jasmine learned that actions were far more important than words and she decided that she was never going to doubt herself ever again.

It's great to believe in yourself and in your newly acquired abilities. Having confidence in yourself is important, as long as it isn't misplaced or at the expense of others.

Jasmine struggled with her self-belief and this caused her to undervalue herself. Only, when an opportunity arose for her to test out her new skills, she was the only one of her friends who remained calm enough to take control of the situation.

Remember to always believe in your own abilities but not to be arrogant—and to trust in yourself without being doubtful.

You're an amazing girl who cherishes new skills, encourages your worried friends, and helps out others when needed.

Never lose faith in yourself or your abilities. Never forget to sparkle, as you've got this.

CASSIE MAKES A MISJUDGE

When meeting someone for the first time it's easy to make judgments about them solely based on their clothing, age, and hairstyle.

We all talk differently, hold ourselves differently, and act differently but it's important to remember that looks can be deceiving.

That nervous, quiet boy on the quiz team actually knows all of the answers.

The vibrant lady with rainbow hair loves to bake for her friends and family.

The moody-looking girl in the big stomping boots is actually just lonely and longs to make friends.

We never truly know what someone is like until we take the time to get to know them. By making presumptions based entirely on another person's appearance, we might end up missing out on getting to know someone amazing.

For Cassie, no weekend was complete without a visit to the local park.

She adored standing on the pebbled surface next to the pond and feeding the ducks.
Skipping along the flowerbed-bordered path.

And enjoying her ice cream on the bench beneath the majestic maple tree.

But most of all, she loved playing on the castle-themed playground.

On this particular day, Cassie and her best friend Lea had just finished feeding the ducks and were about to go to the playground when they spotted someone peculiar…

There was an old lady wearing a long tatty gray dress, an ill-fitted moth-eaten coat, and a worn-out hat with some feathers pinned to it.

Cassie didn't know what to make of this old lady's strange appearance and she couldn't help but glance over at her warily. The old lady smiled at Cassie, then mumbled to herself as she placed her gloved hands on the frame of her bag and then wheeled it up the path.

"Come on, let's go and play," Lea pulled on Cassie's sweater.

"Uhm yep, sure," she replied, as she gave a cautious look over at the spot where the strange woman had just been.

Cassie tried to shrug off her unease, then followed Lea along the flower-bordered path toward the playground. Once there, she chased her friend into the wooden fortress and whizzed down the slide.

"I'm the queen of the castle," Lea shouted, as she peered over the side of the wooden tower. "You can't catch me," she giggled before she ran off along the rope bridge.

"Yes, I ca-" Cassie turned her head to the side of the park, then she froze in panic.

There, standing by the side of the path was the scary old lady. She continued to mumble to herself as she picked a candy wrapper off the ground and stuffed it in her pocket.

"What's wrong?" Lea came up behind Cassie and caused her to jump.

"I… Uhm… What do you think she's doing here?" Cassie gave a curious glare over at the old lady who was now talking to a sparrow.

"It looks like she's making friends," Lea chuckled. "Come on, let's go on the big swing," she grabbed her hand and led her across the playground.

Suddenly, a loud yapping sound echoed toward them, followed by a shout:

"ROVER!"

Both girls stared in pure terror as a large, shaggy brown and white dog leaped toward them, its teeth barred.

"ROVER, NO!" the frantic owner yelled, as he desperately ran after it.

Cassie and Lea grabbed onto each other and trembled in fright. Not knowing what else to do, Cassie shut her eyes. She could still hear the owner's panicked shouts and the tapping of the dog's lead as it trailed behind it.

She expected the dog to leap up at her—only it didn't!

She cautiously opened one eye to see what was happening. To her surprise, she saw the old lady standing in between them and the dog, its lead tightly clutched in her grasp.

"Don't worry girls, I'll sort this," she said, as she turned to address the panting owner, who'd just caught up with them.

"Here!" she thrust the dog's lead into his hands. "Keep a firm hold of it next time or don't bring it here again," she jabbed a finger against his chest. "I won't have any trouble in my park."

27

The owner flustered out a string of apologies, then he bowed his head in remorse, as he led the dog away.

The old lady turned to the two girls and her stern demeanor instantly changed to one of warmth.

"Sweeties, are you both alright?" she said in a kind voice.

Both girls exchanged surprised looks, then nodded at the old lady.

"That pesky dog and his bad owner. How dare they cause havoc in my park," she mumbled to herself.

"T-thank you for s-saving us," Cassie trembled out. "Uhm… I-it's your park?"

"No need to thank me, and yes, it's mine of a sort. You see, I live in it, and I like to keep it tidy and safe."

"You live in this park? But don't you get cold?" Lea said in surprise.

"Yes sweetie, I live here. And yes, sometimes it can be rather teeth-chattering," she shuddered as she spoke. "I better be off. You girls take care now."

The girls waved at the old lady as she hummed a tune to herself as she pushed her bag up the path. As she watched her leave, Cassie felt terrible for misjudging her and she wished there was something she could do to thank her.

...

Back at home, a confused Cassie opened up to her mom about what'd happened in the park.

"I shouldn't have misjudged the old lady just because she's different," she said, as she twirled her straw around her glass of lemonade.

"Cassie, my sweet girl, please don't feel bad," she gave her a warm smile. "Sometimes it's easy to jump to the wrong conclusion about someone. But today you've learned that the person we least expect may just turn out to have the brightest of hearts."

"I know," she sighed. "I just wish there was a way I could thank her."

"Perhaps there is a way of doing that," her mom's lips curled into a knowing smile. "Is there a particular item you think this lady would appreciate?"

Cassie stuck out her bottom lip in thought. Then her eyes widened when an idea popped into her mind.

"Well, there is something but it will need a bit of a clean and patch-up first."

"In that case, we better get started then," her mom smiled.

Cassie quickly pushed back her chair and ran up to her room to get the item in question. As she stared down at the well-loved but still in good condition mint green blanket, she felt sure that the old lady would make good use of it.

Cassie stayed up late preparing her gift for the old lady. With her mom's help, she washed the blanket in lavender-scented detergent and patched up the small hole and loose threads. As she stared down at the newly improved blanket, she felt proud of herself for doing this kind deed.

The next day she entered the park with her mom and searched around for the old lady. It wasn't long before she found her sitting on a bench close to the pond and talking to a duck.

Cassie let go of her mom's hand and skipped across the pebbled surface toward her.

"Hello sweetie. It's nice to see you again," the old lady gave her a gummy smile, and then she readjusted her hat.

At first, Cassie felt too nervous to talk but after looking over at her mom and receiving a nod of reassurance, she took a deep breath and then smiled at the old lady.

"I got you this… as a thank you," she nervously held the neatly folded blanket out to her. "I, uhm, washed it and sewed it up myself."

"For me?" She carefully took the blanket from Cassie and peered down in pleased surprise.

"Ahh, it's lovely."

"It's to keep you warm at night. It was my old one but I have two so I thought you might like it."

"Yes, I do. I like it very much," she held the blanket up to her nose and inhaled its scent. "Mmm lavender, my favorite. Thank you, sweetie, that's very kind of you."

After that, the old lady took a handful of seeds out of her pocket and handed some of them to Cassie, who smiled sweetly at her as they fed the ducks together.

As she waved the old lady goodbye, Cassie made a promise to herself that from that day onward she wasn't going to judge someone just on their appearance ever again.

It's easy to make assumptions about people who look and act differently from us. You might think they're odd, crazy, or strange.

But just as Cassie learned, we don't really know what someone is like until we take the time to get to know them.

When you next meet someone you aren't too sure about, remember to give them a fair chance before being too quick to judge them. You never know, it might just lead to you making a fantastic new friend.

ELOISE EMBRACES HER BRACES

Sometimes, making little changes to your appearance can be a lot of fun. This could be trying a different hairstyle, adding some cute new pieces to your wardrobe, or testing a new hairstyle.

Other times, you may have to experience a change that doesn't seem quite so fun, such as having braces fitted or wearing glasses.

It's natural for changes that are out of your control to make you feel a little bit uncertain and afraid. You may worry that your friends will see you differently and that they might not accept this new version of you.

It's important to remember that your friends like you because you're a kind, caring, sweet girl— a change in your appearance won't alter how amazing your friends think you are.

Eloise sat in the large cushioned dentist chair and looked at the poster of smiling teeth on the wall in front of her.

She didn't mind coming here for her yearly check-up, as the dentist, Mr. Goodwin was a friendly man who always complimented her teeth. Then at the end of her appointment, she got to pick a sticker from the glass bowl.

"All done," Mr. Goodwin said as he placed his tools down on the tray and addressed both her and her mom. "Eloise, it's clear you've been taking great care of your teeth—but now that you've lost most of your baby teeth, I believe it's the right time for you to get braces to align them fully. I'll refer you to an orthodontist."

Eloise felt her heart sink at the mention of that word.

Braces! She had to get braces!

She didn't want braces. No one else in her class had them yet and she didn't want to be the only one. What if everyone thought this was sooo uncool and teased her about it? What if they no longer wanted to be her friend?

As she followed her mom out of the room, she held her head low and dragged her feet. The smiley dentist assistant held the bowl of stickers out to her but all she noticed was how perfect and braces-free her teeth were.

"I hope you pick a good one," she said warmly, her perfect-toothed smile widening.

Eloise just sighed, and instead of taking great care in which sticker she picked like she usually did; she just grabbed the first one her fingers fumbled over, and then she walked out of the room.

The next day at school Eloise didn't tell any of her friends about her impending braces. She wanted to feel normal for as long as possible, so she tried to put her worries about getting braces to the back of her mind.

Only as time went on, the big day grew closer and closer until it eventually arrived.

In the orthodontist waiting room, she took one last look in the mirror at her brace-free mouth— she liked the way she looked now and she didn't want anything to change. She thought it was so unfair that she had to have braces fitted, and she wished more than anything that her teeth would magically align by themselves.

…

"Sweetie, they'll take a little bit of getting used to, that's all," her mom said in a gentle voice.

They were on the car ride back from the orthodontist and Eloise's mouth felt clunky and strange. She didn't reply to her mom as her mouth felt too numb and odd to talk. So, she just gave a reluctant nod and then stared out of the window.

This morning she'd felt like a normal girl, and now she felt like the odd one out.

Back at home, she concluded that having braces was no fun at all. When she looked in the bathroom mirror and saw her lilac bands staring back at her, even them being in her favorite color didn't alter the fact that she hated them, and she now hated her smile.

When she ate broccoli for dinner, she got bits of it stuck in her braces and had to use floss to remove them.

She kept on accidentally knocking her tongue against the metal in her mouth which reminded her how uncool and glum she felt.

Worse still, it was school tomorrow, which meant she had to go into the classroom and have everyone gawp at her braces. The fear of this built up in Eloise's mind, so when her mom asked her to get her schoolbag ready for tomorrow, she burst into tears.

"I'm not going to school. You can't make me," she sobbed, as she stormed past her mom and shut herself in the bathroom.

She sat in the empty tub and pulled the shower curtain across so that she didn't catch a glimpse of her braces in the mirror. She was adamant that she was just going to stay here in this bathroom and NEVER go to school again, well, at least not until her teeth were aligned and she didn't have to wear braces anymore.

A soft knock sounded on the door, and her mom's worried voice said:

"El, are you okay in there?"

"No!" Go away," she shouted through her sobs.

"El, please tell me what's wrong? Is this about your braces?"

39

"Yes, I hate them. They look stupid and feel funny, and everyone at school is going to laugh at me."

"Sweetie, why would anyone do that?" her mom asked.

"Because no one else has to wear braces. Only me."

"So what?! You don't laugh at your friends for their differences, do you?"

Eloise thought hard about her friends and what made them different from her. Hailie had an inhaler for her asthma, and Luca wore blue-framed glasses. She never laughed at her friends about these things, and if she was curious about anything then she just asked her friends about them.

"No, I guess not. But I'd still rather not go to school until my braces are removed," she sighed.

Eventually, with some more soothing words, her mom managed to calm Eloise down and persuade her to open the door. Then she led her into the living room and they both cuddle up under a fluffy blanket on the couch.

"Sweetie, I don't want you worrying about tomorrow. Your friends all like you and think you're great. Braces won't change that."

"But how can you be so sure?" she looked up at her mom with worried eyes.

"Let me tell you a story about me, it took place when I was the age you are now," she gently readjusted her arm around her daughter. "I loved to climb trees so I could sneakily drop a water balloon on your Uncle Jamie. One day I was perched in a tree waiting for him to appear when I misplaced my footing and fell onto the ground. I broke my arm and had to have this horrible, big, itchy cast put on it. I hated it and worried all my friends would laugh at me."

"And… did they?" she asked curiously.

"No, actually it was quite the opposite. They asked lots of questions about the cast, signed it with kind messages and drawings, and carried my lunch tray for me."

"That was very nice of them but a cast is cool, while braces are awful," she let out a downbeat sigh.

"Back then I thought my cast was awful too but my friends didn't seem to think so," her mom chuckled to herself, then continued; "it made me realize that I was silly for wasting so much time and energy on worrying in the first place. It's our differences that make us, us. Your friends think you're great and this isn't going to change just because you have braces now, is it?"

"I suppose not," Eloise muttered, then she snuggled closer to her mom.

42

She still felt nervous about going to school tomorrow but she knew that she couldn't hide away at home forever. She also had to admit that a part of her really wanted to see her friends—she just hoped that they would be accepting of her now her appearance had changed.

....

The next day Eloise walked down to breakfast feeling nervous and apprehensive. As she stirred her spoon around her bowl of soggy cereal, her mom gave her a reassuring look.

"Sweetie, it will be okay. All you need to do is be your usual confident, friendly self and show your braces off with pride."

Eloise knew her mom was right—so what if she had braces now, she was still her, and having braces didn't change that.

"Do I have any cereal stuck in my braces?" she showed her mom her teeth.

"No, you're all good," she chuckled.

Eloise flicked her tongue over her braces when suddenly a great idea popped into her head.

"One minute, mom," she said, as she whizzed out of the kitchen and ran upstairs to get something important.

When she reappeared, she was wearing a lilac sweater the exact color of her braces.

"Sweetie, you're matching," her mom smiled on seeing her.

Eloise grinned at her mom. She might not have had much say in having braces but the one thing she did have a say on was what color they would be.

...

Eloise arrived in class and immediately sat at her desk in silence. Her friends greeted her but she stayed silent and managed a weak smile without opening her mouth.

They gave her confused looks and continued chatting amongst themselves. As Eloise sat there, she remembered what her mom said about being confident in who she is. So, she took a deep breath, looked at her friends, and gave them a big, lilac smile.

"Oh wow, I didn't know you were getting braces," Ivy said in surprise.

"I love the color and how you've matched it to your sweater," Hailie smiled at her. "Did getting them fitted hurt?"

"No, they just feel a little uncomfortable but I'm starting to get used to them," Eloise replied in a friendly manner.

"Did it take ages to fit them?" Luca asked.

"About an hour, the orthodontist cleaned my teeth first, then applied this sticky gel to them."

As Eloise's friends continued to ask her lots of questions, she realized something… no one was laughing at her, instead, they all seemed really curious about her braces just like her mom said they would be.

Then at recess, she was walking toward the playground when Ivy caught up with her. Eloise could tell Ivy was nervous by her hesitant look and the way she was chewing on her fingernails.

"I, um, I'm getting braces soon and I'm, um, really scared about it. Does it honestly not hurt?" she asked.

"Nope, it didn't hurt at all. It is a little strange at first but I'm not noticing it so much now."

"Oh, that's good," Ivy managed a small smile. "I hope I get to pick a color. I really want pink… no, purple… no, pink."

"You can pick whatever color bands you want, you can have multiple colors, not just one. Also, you can change these when you go for a check-up."

"Really? Wow, that's sooo cool," Ivy's worried expression transformed into a grin. "In that case, I'm definitely picking pink and purple to start, then I'm going to style my clothes to match like you have."

"That sounds awesome."

"Thanks El, I don't feel so worried anymore," Ivy beamed at her.

"No problem. If you have any more questions, just ask me," she smiled at her friend.

As she watched Ivy skip off happily, she felt good that her kind words and advice had helped reassure her.

She quickly popped into the restroom but as she headed toward an empty cubicle, she caught her reflection in the mirror above the sink. Then she did something she hadn't done since getting her braces—she gave a big, lilac-banded smile at herself.

Eloise realized that she didn't actually mind her braces that much anymore—and she found herself thinking about what color bands she could go for next and how to style her outfits accordingly.

A change to your appearance may seem scary at first and may take some getting used to but it doesn't change the wonderful person you are inside.

Eloise learned that having braces was nowhere near as scary as she thought it would be and that her friends were very curious and understanding about it. She even ended up reassuring her worried friend.

You are a kind, caring, special girl, and differences in your appearance or routine won't change this.

Always remember that your differences don't change the glow in your heart and the skip in your step—they just make them bigger and brighter.

47

AMELIA'S KICK FOR COURAGE

Talking to people we know, such as our family and friends is easy but sometimes in life, we find ourselves in situations where we have to speak to people we don't know—this often doesn't feel quite so easy!

Whether this is to ask for directions or to pay for something, the thought of talking to a stranger might make you feel shy or nervous.

It's normal to feel this way about talking to someone you don't know but if you don't find the courage to speak to that new person then you might find yourself lost and confused, or unable to buy the item you really want.

As scary as approaching someone new may seem, please remember that they're people just like you are and chances are they feel a little nervous too.

So next time you're feeling shy about a situation remember that you're a friendly, caring, amazing girl who can do anything you put your mind to.

It was a sunny but breezy day in the park, and Amelia was dribbling her purple and black soccer ball across the grass. Her friend, Kirstin, moved in a crab-like fashion between the sweater and water bottle they were using as goal marks.

Thinking fast, Amelia came up on the right-hand side, passed her ball from one foot to the other, then kicked the ball toward the inside of the goal marks. Kristin dived to the side but the ball flew over the top of her hands, through the goal markers, and then it slowed down and came to a stop in a bush.

49

"She shoots. She scores. She wins. And that's a sensational goal from newcomer, Amelia Thorne," she said in her best announcer's voice, as she slid to her knees and lifted her arms in the air.

"You just got lucky," Kristin remarked, as she walked over with the ball now clutched under her arm.

"Yeah, yeah, if you say so," Amelia grinned at her friend.

Amelia's love of soccer began at a young age when her toddler self would often be caught sneakily taking the dog's ball and kicking it around the house.

When she got a little older her parents signed her up for the local girls' soccer team, and that's where she met Kristin. Not only did both girls share a devoted love of the sport but they both dreamed of becoming one of the next great midfielders just like Rose Lavelle or Lindsay Horan.

"Let's see if you can beat that outstanding feat of goalscoring," Amelia said, as she took her place in the makeshift goal.

Kristin gave a concentrated face as she tapped her foot over the ball. Then suddenly, she began dribbling it forward, performed an air-spinning trick called a roulette, then kicked the ball with great force toward the goal.

Amelia darted toward the ball but it seemed to get higher and faster…

Until suddenly it was zooming over the wooden park fence and into someone's backyard.

Both girls gasped in shock, then shared dumbfounded looks.

"I'm sorry, Amelia. I didn't mean to kick it that hard," Kristin said coyly.

"It's okay. I know it was an accident," Amelia sighed. "But what do we do now?"

"It must have gone in the yard of the house behind the park. You can knock on the door and ask for it back," Kristin suggested.

"Me! Why ME?!" Amelia shook her head in fear. "You're the one who kicked it over the fence, so you should go get it back."

"Knock on a stranger's door? No! N-no way!" Kristin's voice trembled with nerves. "I-it's just a ball. Let's just leave it there."

The thought of leaving the ball behind made Amelia feel overwhelmed with sadness. To her, it wasn't just any old ball—it was the extra special ball her mom had gifted her for her last birthday.

The thought of returning home and explaining to her mom that she'd been too afraid to ask for it back, made her feel awful.

"Fine! I'll do it," Amelia said with an assertive nod. "But… you have to come to the door with me."

"I—um—fine," Kristin gave a reluctant nod. "But I'm not doing any of the talking."

Both girls gathered their belongings and then followed the fence perimeter out of the park and around to the row of houses that backed onto it. They both stopped in front of a house with a blue door.

Amelia took a deep breath and tried to remain calm. She was trembling and sweating with nerves and the more she thought about knocking on a stranger's door, the more panic rose inside of her and made her want to run.

"Come on, Amelia. You can do this," Kristin gave her a gentle shove forward.

"Pfft, that's easy for you to say. You're not the one doing the talking." She turned around and gave her friend a stern look.

Taking another deep breath, she began to walk forward, and Kristin cautiously followed behind her.

The closer she got to the blue door the more afraid she became, and the more frantic her thoughts grew. A dozen questions buzzed through her mind—what if the owner was mean and slammed the door in her face? What if they claimed the ball had squashed their flowerbed and insisted she pays for damages?

Amelia bravely stepped up to the blue door and then stared at it. She told herself she needed to stop catastrophizing the situation. Then she reminded herself what her dear grandma told her: *"Sweetie, you can't expect to receive what you never ask for, can you?"*

With her grandma's wise words at the forefront of her mind, Amelia reached out and knocked on the door. She moved from foot to foot as she waited anxiously. Then, just when she was about to turn around and walk off, the door swung open, and a teenage girl looked up from her phone screen and glared at Amelia.

"Yeah, what?" she said in an abrupt voice before she looked back at her phone.

"I, um, my ball," she took a deep breath and willed herself to calm down. "I'm sorry to bother you but my ball is in your yard. Please can we get it back?"

"Yeah, whatever you want. This way," she didn't divert her gaze as she stepped past the girls, and with the briefest of hand waves, she gestured them to follow her.

Amelia and Kirstin shared dubious looks as they sidled up to each other.

"What if there's a scary dog back there? Or worse… an angry adult?" Kristin whispered.

"I'll take my chances, as I want my ball back," Amelia took a brave step ahead of her friend and followed the girl through the gate and into the backyard; a worried Kristin reluctantly followed behind her.

When both girls saw that there was neither a scary dog nor any angry adults about, they both felt much better—in fact, the only new person standing in the enormous backyard complete with a football net was a girl around their age. Even better, she was wearing a soccer shirt and gripping Amelia's beloved purple and black soccer ball.

"Hello," the girl looked at them curiously. "Can I help you?"

"They want their ball back, obviously," the teenage girl rolled her eyes. "Urgh! I don't understand soccer," she muttered under her breath as she started to walk back toward the gate.

"Don't mind her, she thinks soccer's a waste of time and only cares about watching stupid videos on her phone. Not me though, I think soccer is the best thing ever," the girl grinned at them, as she held the ball out to Amelia.

"Us too," she took the ball from her with a smile. "We both want to be famous midfielders when we're older."

"Really? That's my dream too, I think Rose Lavelle is the coolest."

"I love Rose Lavelle," Amelia smiled.

"Do you both want to play a game? Oh, I'm Nicole by the way."

Both Amelia and Kristin nodded in response, then they introduced themselves to Nicole. After that, all three girls had an amazing time playing soccer together.

Amelia felt proud of herself for facing her fears and talking to a stranger. Not only did it lead her to get her beloved ball back but because of her courage and determination, it also led both her and Kirstin to make a great new friend.

The thought of talking to someone you don't know may seem like a scary thing to do.

It's normal for this to leave us with a swirling, nervous feeling in our tummies. But sometimes just like Amelia, we find ourselves in situations where to achieve our goals, we first have to speak to someone new.

Showing courage not only led Amelia to get her ball back but also to feelings of accomplishment, pride, happiness, and best of all, she ended up with an awesome new friend.

OLIVIA WANTS THAT ONE

You know that feeling when you want something so badly that it seems to be on a constant, beaming, cartwheeling, loop in your mind?

Of course you do, as every single one of us feels like this sometimes.

When you long for something this badly then it's normal to create a dreamlike world in your imagination where having this certain thing makes everything seem so much brighter.

Suddenly, not having it may feel like the worst thing in the world.

Getting what you want can be fantastic but sometimes getting something else instead may just lead to some amazing surprises.

The new toy given to you for your birthday may not flash different colors but turns out it spins and flips instead—cool.

The school art club is full but there's an opening in the photography club which catches your attention—snap!

There's no honeycomb ice cream left but this leads you to try the white chocolate sprinkles flavor—yum!

Not getting what we think we want might just lead us to discover something far more fun, challenging, and exciting.

Life isn't always predictable and sometimes it may feel unfair but it's the unpredictable surprises that often end up leading us to those unexpected magical moments.

Olivia liked to perform.

She thrived off the excited tingling feeling she felt when she stepped on stage.

She loved dressing up in different costumes.

She adored receiving rapturous applause from the audience.

So when her teacher, Miss Hamilton, announced to the class they'd be doing a stage production of *Alice in Wonderland,* Olivia was certain the part of Alice would be hers.

At lunchtime, she sat at a table with her best friend Emma and excitedly talked about the play.

"I can't wait to play Alice. I wonder what the dress will be like?" she said dreamily, as pulled the crust off her sandwich. "Emma, you'll make a great white rabbit or dormouse, so you should audition for those parts."

Emma gave a flustered look as she stared down at her half-eaten apple.

"Um, actually, I'm going to audition for the part of Alice too," she looked up and gave her friend an awkward smile. "That is okay, isn't it?"

Olivia's eyes widened in surprise. She didn't expect to hear this from her quiet, more reserved friend.

"Sure, you can audition for any part you like," she gave an aloof shrug, then bit into her sandwich.

…

As soon as Olivia arrived home from school, she spread the script out on her bed, highlighted all of Alice's lines in pink, then spent hours learning them.

She practiced her Alice expressions and mannerisms in her bedroom mirror.

She allocated her family different parts and made them practice with her.

She even watched the movie version so she could further understand the character.

Olivia was adamant that no one else had put as much effort into preparing for this part as she had, and that the role was guaranteed to be hers.

…

Audition day arrived, and Olivia took a center spot on the stage, and confidently performed her lines.

Everyone else's auditions were good, including Emma's, but she believed they weren't as great as hers was.

As Miss Hamilton gathered the class around her and was about to allocate the roles, Olivia felt certain her name would be called for the lead.

"You've all done amazingly and you've all impressed me greatly. Every one of these parts is crucial to make the play work," Miss Hamilton smiled, as she peered around at everyone. "I've decided that the part of Alice will go to… Emma."

As Olivia stared at a shocked-looking Emma she couldn't hide her dismay. What! There must have been a mistake. Alice was her part, not Emma's. She was a much more confident actress than she was and she deserved that part over her.

"Olivia, I think you'll be just perfect as the Queen of Hearts," Miss Hamilton said to her.

Olivia gulped back in confusion. She hadn't even auditioned for that part, so it made no sense to her that she'd been chosen for it. She wanted to be the lead, not some supporting role.

Her bad mood continued, as she watched the other children gather around Emma and congratulate her. Then Emma caught her eye and walked over to her.

"Well done, you'll be just perfect as the Queen of Hearts," she smiled and went to hug her.

"Pfft! I'm a far better actress than you, this is stupid," she jerked away from her friend, then stormed off.

This wasn't fair and she decided if she couldn't be the part she wanted to play then she wouldn't be in this stupid play at all.

...

At home, Olivia slumped down on the couch and stared with folded arms, and a sour face at the blank TV screen.

Her big sister walked into the room and gave a confused look from the TV to Olivia.

"I find it helps if you turn it on first," she chuckled but Olivia's demeanor didn't falter. "Um, sis, what's wrong?"

"I didn't get the lead… Emma did! I'm stuck being the stupid Queen of Hearts!"

"The Queen of Hearts isn't a stupid role at all; it's actually a pretty important part," she said, as she sat down next to Olivia.

"But it's not the part I wanted!" she exclaimed. "I'm not doing it! I'm pulling out of the play!"

"Are you sure you want to do that?" her sister arched her brow. "We don't always get what we want in life but do you really want to let your classmates down because of this?"

"No one will care, it's not as if I'm playing Alice," she huffed.

"I don't think that's true. All the parts are important in their own way and clearly your teacher cast you as the Queen of Hearts because she thinks you'll bring something awesome to the part," she placed her arm around Olivia and pulled her in for a sideways hug.

Olivia stuck out her bottom lip as she gave this some thought.

"Also think about how awful Emma will feel if you drop out of the play?" Sophie gave her a questioning look, then she continued. "If you'd been given the part and Emma acted like you were doing now, how would you feel? Not great, huh?"

Olivia stuck out her bottom lip as she gave this some thought. She decided that maybe she had been a little unfair to Emma and she wanted to put it right.

...

It was the first play rehearsal and Olivia walked into the room holding her script and walked straight over to Emma and tapped her on the shoulder.

"I just wanted to say well done on getting the part, you'll make a great Alice. Sorry I was a grouch about it yesterday," she said.

"That's okay. I think you'll be great at your part too," Emma smiled at her.

Olivia still wasn't sure if she liked the part she'd been given but regardless of this, she decided to heed her sister's advice and give it a chance. So, she spent the next few weeks learning her lines, walking around in a queen-like stance, and coming out with the phrase: *Off with their heads,* at every given opportunity.

As time went by, something unexpected began to happen… Olivia found herself enjoying her part far more than she thought she would. Best of all, she adored her costume, which was a beautiful black and red dress with embellished hearts on it, and a pointed gold crown.

It was the last rehearsal before the big performance and Olivia and her classmates were waiting in the rehearsal room for the teacher to arrive. As she peered around the room, she noticed that Emma wasn't there yet. This was odd, as she was normally a very punctual person.

Suddenly Miss Hamilton walked in with a flustered look on her face.

"Class, I'm afraid Emma is sick and won't be able to perform in the play tomorrow. Olivia, Mina, and Cleo, why don't you three all read out the lines?" she looked at each of the girls.

Olivia peered down at the script but then she flipped it over and continued to read out Alice's lines off by heart. Miss Hamilton seemed very impressed with both her excellent memory and strong performance.

"Olivia, would you like to be Alice?" she asked her.

Olivia gulped back and then nervously fiddled with the corner of her script. She'd longed for this part more than anything else but now she felt a knot in her stomach where her excitement should be.

The character of Alice was quiet to the Queen of Heart's loud, polite to her brash, and good-hearted to her self-centeredness.

Olivia found herself identifying more with Alice but where was the fun in playing a character she was most like? Being the Queen of Hearts was a challenge that she'd found herself embracing. She now realized that the best part about performing was that she could become a role opposite to her true self.

"I, um, thank you Miss but I want to stick with my part as I find it more fun and challenging to play."

The teacher accepted Olivia's decision and picked one of the other girls to fill in as Alice.

As excited as Olivia was about the play, she also felt sad that her best friend wouldn't be able to perform alongside her. She knew how much work Emma had put into this play and it seemed so unfair that she wouldn't get a chance to shine on stage.

She decided that she wanted to cheer her friend up, so that afternoon when she arrived home, she asked her sister to help her put together a basket containing some of Emma's favorite things. She added some chocolate buttons, cherry lip candies, a glitter pad, scented gel pens, a cute kitten teddy, and a handmade 'get well soon' card which she'd decorated with colorful stickers.

Olivia and her sister walked over to Emma's house and handed the basket to her mom who thanked them kindly and told them she would go and give it to Emma right away.

On the walk home, Olivia couldn't stop thinking about the play, and she excitedly practiced her lines with her sister.

By not getting the part she wanted she'd ended up with a part that she found far more enjoyable and challenging to play.

You really, really, REALLY wanted that one thing… but you didn't get it!

Hmm, this can feel frustrating but Olivia didn't get what she wanted either.

Once Olivia stopped focusing on what she didn't have and instead focused on the part she'd been given, she ended up realizing that it was perfect for her.

If we spend so much time lingering on what we didn't get instead of concentrating on what we did, we might end up missing out on a truly amazing opportunity.

So next time you don't get what you thought you wanted, focus on what you have instead. After all, the best things in life have a way of finding us when we least expect them.

AVA'S KINDNESS SHINES THROUGH

Showing kindness toward others can be as simple as a warm smile, a friendly wave, or a welcoming hello.

These gestures may seem small but they can make a BIG difference to someone's day.

70

Being kind to someone when other people are being mean to them isn't always easy. It's normal to want to shrink in size and stay out of the way.

You don't have to shout to be noticed— all you have to do is just be you, and your caring, thoughtful nature will shine through.

Never forget how sweet, thoughtful and kind you are. You are an amazing girl who can make those around you sparkle as brightly as you do.

When Ava arrived in her classroom, ready for a fun day of learning and being around her friends, she noticed an unfamiliar face talking to the teacher.

As she lined her pen, pencil, ruler, and eraser out in front of her, she found that she kept on glancing over at this new girl, who was restlessly chewing on her lip as the teacher continued talking to her.

"She looks frightened," her friend Elodie whispered to her.

"I hope she's okay," Ava replied.

Looking over at the nervous-looking girl reminded Ava of how afraid she'd felt on her first day at this school. She hoped that the new girl would soon settle in and feel less worried.

"Good morning class," Mrs. Forrester, the teacher addressed the class with a warm smile. "This is Harper, she's new. Please can you all make her feel welcome?"

Ava gave Harper a big smile, she just started to smile back when suddenly, the teacher led her over to a middle table where two girls and a boy were sitting.

"Oh no!" Ava thought to herself, as she watched the teacher instruct Harper to sit down next to a brown-haired girl wearing a sparkly pink headband— Michaela.

Ava gulped back and exchanged worried looks with Elodie and her other friends Freddie and Tom. Michaela may have fooled the teacher with her angelic smile but the truth was she was actually a mean girl.

She hoped that Michaela would be different this time but as soon as the teacher left the room to talk to the principal, she glanced over at the new girl and saw Michaela snatch her pencil case from her and begin to riffle through it.

This annoyed Ava so much that she couldn't concentrate on her exercise sheet. She didn't understand why Michaela had to be such a mean girl.

...

During lunchtime, Ava was sitting with her friends, when suddenly Freddie elbowed her in the arm to get her attention.

"Look," he pointed to the other side of the room where Harper was looking very glum as she sat alone. "Shall we invite her to join us?"

"That's a great idea, I'll go and ask her," Ava jumped to her feet and hurried across the room— but before she could reach her, something happened.

Michaela plonked herself down next to Harper and reached across and grabbed the pudding off her tray. Harper tried grabbing it back but Michaela smirked as she held it out of reach. Eventually, Harper gave up, and she ran out of the cafeteria.

Ava watched on with furious eyes, as Michaela began shoveling spoonfuls of Harper's pudding into her mouth. Then she waved her friends over to join her at the table. Ava wandered back to her friends feeling deflated about the situation. She felt terrible for Harper and she hoped that she was okay.

Out in the playground, during a game of chase, Ava was running around the skipping children when sobbing sounds brought her to an abrupt stop. Michaela and her friends were circling someone. As she peered through the gap, she saw that it was an upset-looking Harper.

"You're such a crybaby," Michaela sniggered at her.

"Yeah, you're a stupid crybaby," another boy jeered.

"Go back to the school you came from. No one wants you here," Michaela jibed, and all of her friends laughed.

Suddenly, Harper burst past them and ran off in a cloud of sobs and tears.

"Wait!" Ava shouted after her. "Harper, stop."

But it was too late—Harper had disappeared.

Ava gave it some thought, then concluded that there was only one place in this school where someone this upset would go; the restrooms.

She walked into the girl's restroom and gently called:

"Harper, are you okay?"

"Go away," a sobbing voice came from the far cubicle.

Ava walked over to the cubicle door and in a caring voice, started talking to Harper.

"Please don't be upset. Michaela is mean to everyone, she's just a mean girl."

"Then why did the teacher make me sit by her?" Harper asked through sobs.

"Mrs. Forrester thinks that Michaela is an angel. She's not though, she's really mean."

"B-but she's not like that to anyone else. J-just me!"

"No, that's not true. When I started this school, she was mean to me too," Ava's voice fell quiet as she reminisced.

"Really… but what happened?" she asked in a curious voice.

"I made some great new friends. Now, Michaela doesn't really bother me anymore."

"I miss my friends," Harper said glumly.

"I know. But you can be friends with me and my friends if you'd like"?

There was a brief pause, followed by the sound of a bolt unlocking. Harper opened the door with a tear-stained face and through her sadness, she smiled at Ava.

On the way back to class, Ava asked Harper lots of questions. She found out that they were both proud owners of ginger tabby cats, adored raspberry-flavored candy, longed to own a bright orange bike with a bell, and loved any films that contained talking animals.

Ava also found out that Harper loved to sing and dreamed of becoming a famous pop star like Selena Gomez. Although Ava didn't see herself as much of a singer, she enjoyed listening to pop music and couldn't wait to have Harper around for a cat cuddling, raspberry candy snacking, pop tunes playing, *The Fox and the Hound* watching sleepover.

Back in class, Harper looked terrified as she reluctantly walked over to a smirking Michaela who took delight in patting the space next to her in a taunting fashion. Knowing that she needed to do something about this, Ava spoke to the teacher and explained to her that she'd just befriended Harper and she believed she'd feel more comfortable sitting at a table with her and her friends.

Mrs. Forrester glanced over at Harper and witnessed her flinching nervously, as Michaela smacked her ruler on the table in front of her. She swooped in and told Michaela off for being unkind, then she moved Harper onto a table with Ava and her friends.

From that moment onward, as Harper's confidence began to grow, Michaela's mean comments became less frequent. Ava adored seeing her new friend smile with happiness, and she felt great joy knowing that by showing kindness and support she'd helped make this happen.

Then one day Ava spotted a flyer for the school talent show. Knowing how much Harper longed to be a pop star, at lunchtime, she placed the flyer down in front of a dazed-looking Harper, who immediately stopped drinking her apple juice and stared down at the flyer with terror.

"You have to enter—you'll be amazing," she tried persuading her.

"What! You mean to go on stage! Alone! With all those people watching me! No, no I can't!" she shuddered nervously.

"You have to do it. You're too talented not to," Tom said.

"B-but I can't do it alone," she gave an adamant shake of her head.

"What if you don't have to be alone?" Elodie commented.

"Yes, we could be your backing singers," Ava gave a wide smile.

She looked at us each of them individually then her worried expression curled into a wide grin. With her friends on stage with her then it didn't seem so scary. So, she happily nodded in agreement.

…

The day of the talent contest arrived and on noticing how nervous Harper looked, Ava led her to a quiet area backstage and handed her a small, pink heart gem.

"It's for luck. I grip it when I'm nervous and it makes me feel less afraid," she smiled at her friend.

"Thank you," Harper gave her a touched look. "But don't you need it?"

"No," she shook her head. "I want you to have it. Besides, if I find I ever need it I can ask to borrow it from my kind friend," she gave a beaming smile.

Clutching the heart gem tightly in her hand, Ava walked alongside her friends onto the stage. She heard whispered chattering from the audience and saw all eyes gawping at her, including Michaela who was sniggering with her friends in the front row.

At first, Harper considered turning around and running off stage but then she looked over at her friends and realized that if she did that, she wouldn't just be letting herself down, but she'd be letting them down too.

As the intro music started playing, she took a deep breath, tapped her thumb against the heart gem, then started singing.

Soon, all whispered chatters stopped and gawped looks turned to stares of awe. Harper owned the room with her beautiful voice.

When the song came to an end the audience rose to their feet and cheered and applauded. Harper blushed with happiness, and her friends rushed over to her and gave her a big hug.

After the show, Harper was enjoying receiving praise from the other children when suddenly she heard a croaked voice behind her. She turned around and saw a flustered-looking Michaela staring at her.

Harper felt her heart thud and her mouth turn dessert dry.

"I just wanted to say that you, um, you sounded great," Michaela mumbled.

"Thanks," Harper replied with a shocked smile.

Ava watched Harper from afar and couldn't help but smile with delight. Seeing her friend conquer her nerves and shine brightly on stage was the best feeling in the world.

By being kind to Harper and showing her friendship and support, Ava not only ended up with a great new friend but she also felt tremendous pride in seeing Harper beat the bullies and transform into the brightest of stars.

Starting something new can be scary — I'm talking knees wobbling, tummy gurgling, palms shaking scary.

It's normal to feel nervous and afraid sometimes but just remember that the world is full of lots of kind, caring people who feel nervous and afraid just like you do.

So, next time you feel nervous about something, never be afraid to open up to someone new and let them get to know how great you are.

And if like Ava, you see someone struggling to settle in, then don't be afraid to let your kindness and warmth shine bright.

You never know, this simple act of kindness could end up transforming someone's day from cloudy into one that dazzles.

KIMBERLEY'S FLIP OF FAITH

Despite all of our hard work and best efforts, some things in life don't quite go to plan.

This could be forgetting your words during the school concert. Grazing your knee during the big race. Or getting the hiccups during your flute recital.

When these unexpected things happen, then sometimes others around us might find them funny. No one likes making mistakes, and no one enjoys being laughed at.

You might decide that this is it! You're never going to risk doing anything that you might fail at ever again! That it's just too scary! So, you're just going to give up!

The problem is, if you let your fears control you and stop you from taking on new challenges, then you'll never achieve anything new.

Don't let the risk of failure cause you to give up on your dreams. Instead, be brave and show who's in charge!

From the very first time that Kimberley somersaulted across the floor mat, she knew that gymnastics was for her.

With the training and support from her coach she was soon doing a back handspring across the mat, a round-off on the vault, and a mill circle on the uneven bars.

But her absolute favorite piece of equipment to perform on was the balance beam. When she was up there, she felt as agile as a cat and as graceful as a bird, and she loved to wow people with her tricky routine.

When it came to performing on the balance beam Kimberley knew she was a natural. So, when her coach suggested she enter a local contest, Kimberley excitedly agreed.

She was halfway through her routine where she'd just performed a spectacular split jump which received numerous gasps from the audience. As she balanced along the beam, her arms outstretched and her body posed, she felt fantastic, she felt incredible…

Then oh no! She felt her foot slip. She tried to save her balance but it was too late and suddenly she was tumbling in a graceless fashion off the beam and landing in a heap on the mat.

Through her thudding heart and panicking mind, she realized something—her ankle was throbbing. It was as she reached out to place her hand on it that she heard it…

Someone laughed!

The problem is, that laughter has a way of being infectious, so as Kimberley's coach helped her hobble off the mat, she heard the gymnasts surrounding her cackle and snicker.

Messing up her routine was bad enough without the other gymnasts laughing at her. At that moment she longed for the floor to open and swallow her up.

…

Time passed and Kimberley's ankle healed. She was soon back doing a front-handspring jump over the vault and tumbling across the mat. She even got back on the balance beam and completed her routine perfectly.

But then one day, after practice, as she was exiting the floor mat, her coach approached her.

"I think you're ready to get back into competing. There's a competition coming up, you should enter."

Kimberley turned pale and started to tremble. Practicing was fine when it was for fun but the thought of performing in front of all those glaring gymnasts and judges made her tummy swish with nerves.

"No thank you. I'm just going to do gymnastics for fun; no more competitions," she replied with an adamant shake of her head.

Her coach sat down on the bench next to the mat and patted the free space next to her. Kimberley sat on the edge of the bench and nervously picked at her fingernails.

"Honey, it sure seems a big shame that you're just going to give up. Especially after all the hard work and practice you've put in," she reached across and gently rubbed Kimberley's arm. "Is there a reason why you feel this way?"

"Maybe," she sighed. "It's, um, it's because of the last competition. I messed up and everyone laughed at me. I don't want that to happen again, it's too scary."

"Kimberley, all gymnasts make mistakes in their routine sometimes. Back in my competing days, I once slipped as I was walking to the vault," she told her with a reminiscing smile. "After that, I developed terrible stage fright and I refused to compete for months afterward."

"You did?" Kimberley looked at her in surprise

"Oh yes. I assure you, it happens to us all," she chuckled. "Sometimes, despite our best efforts, things don't always go to plan. When this happens it's important to learn from these situations and use them to improve and grow."

"But what if I mess up again and everyone makes fun of me?" as she spoke, she felt the panic rise inside of her.

"Hmm, how about you compete in a group on the floor? That way it won't feel so daunting for you?" she suggested.

Kimberley shook her head. She longed to compete again and impress the judges with her skillful routines but being in a team sounded just as scary as performing alone.

"B-but what if I mess up and ruin it for the whole team?" she thought out loud.

"Honey, if we don't take a risk and try again, then we'll always be left wondering what if? And trust me, those what-if moments are far more haunting than the what-were moments," her coach gave her a reassuring smile. "The other girls in the team are all newbies to competitions so you'll be able to motivate and support each other. The contest entry has to be submitted by tomorrow. Why not sleep on it and let me know your decision in the morning?"

Kimberley responded with a single nod. As much as she wanted to enter the contest, she wasn't sure if she was brave enough. Being part of a team was new for her, and it meant she would have to compete on the floor, not her beloved balance beam.

...

That evening, Kimberley couldn't stop thinking about the competition. It played on her mind while she was eating her dinner and caused her to drop a dollop of gravy mash onto the table.

It danced across her thoughts as she tried and failed to concentrate on her favorite cartoon.

It crawled through her daydreams as she got ready for bed and resulted in her putting her pajama top on backward.

Sensing something was wrong, her mom tucked her tightly into bed next to her fluffy bunny teddy, then looked at her with gentle concern and said:

"Kimmy, honey, is something wrong?"

Kimberley chewed on the side of her lip, then she looked into her mom's warm eyes.

"I have to let my coach know by tomorrow if I'm going to enter a group competition or not. I don't know if I'm brave enough to face people. What if I mess up again and cause my team to lose?"

"Oh sweetie, as long as you try your best then it doesn't matter if you do make a mistake. I know my brave girl can handle anything," she leaned over and kissed her on the forehead.

Kimberley didn't feel very brave but she wished more than anything that she could be it.

"Good night, sweetie," her mom smiled over from the doorway.

Kimberley peered at the lilac nightlight on her nightstand. She wanted to perform and shine as brightly and amazingly as that light did. As she rubbed her face against the soft fur of her bunny teddy, she took one last look at the glistening light before she closed her eyes.

...

Kimberley awoke with a start and raced downstairs to use the phone. After considering what both her coach and her mom had said she decided that she didn't want to allow one bad experience to cause her to give up, after all she was a brave and strong girl.

She called her coach and nervously told her to enter her into the competition.

Later that day, when she arrived at the studio for her first team practice session, she saw four nervous-looking girls all sitting on the mat. She smiled at them and sat down next to a particularly frightened-looking girl with pigtails.

"Hi, I'm Emily," the girl smiled anxiously. "This is my first time competing so I'm really nervous."

"I'm Kimberley. I've competed alone before but not in a group. We've got this," she smiled reassuringly at her.

On realizing that she wasn't the only one who had stage fright, Kimberley felt much better. Their first practice session went really well and because Kimberley was the most experienced out of them all, the other girls came to her for tips and advice.

As the practice sessions continued Kimberley felt her confidence growing and she found that her fear began to be replaced with excitement.

When the day of the competition arrived, she put her sparkly outfit on, held her head up high, and confidently walked out onto the mat with her new teammates by her side.

Before the music started, she looked over at her coach and saw her smiling over at her with a big thumbs up. Then she looked at Emily, and they exchanged supportive smiles. Instantly, calmness washed over Kimberley and she forgot about all of the onlookers and focused on the performance.

As soon as she began to perform her nerves trickled away and she lost herself to the moment. The audience seemed to love it and gave impressed gasps for their synchronized front walkovers, cartwheels, and front handsprings.

As she walked off the mat to rapturous applause she had a huge grin on her face, as despite her fears, she had gone out there and performed an amazing routine.

Then, to make things even better the judges announced the results... they'd come in second place.

All of the girls squealed and hugged each other excitedly. As her coach and the other gymnasts came over and congratulated them, Kimberley gleamed with pride.

Looking over at Emily and the other ecstatic girls filled her with joy. She knew that she'd made the right decision to face her fears head-on and never give up.

Sometimes bad experiences happen. These can be annoying, frustrating and most of all, embarrassing.

When something like this happens, then just like Kimberley, giving up might seem like a less scary option than trying again.

It's okay to be upset when you go through a bad experience. But if you dwell on the bad instead

94

of learning from it and growing then you'll never get to experience the excitement when something goes right.

Don't let one bad experience stop you from trying again. Instead, you can use this experience to motivate others who are going through similar fears.

However hard and scary it may seem at times, just remember that you are brave, you are amazing, and you don't give up!!!

COLORING PAGE

IMPRINT

The author is represented by Silviyas Books LTD

Publishing imprint Silvis Books

Contact: info@silvisbooks.com

Publication Year: 2023

ISBN: 979-8-9865737-1-7

Cover illustration: Christina Michalos

Interior images from www.depositphotos.com

Learn more at www.sophiepotterbooks.com

Follow on instagram @SophiePotterBooks

Responsible for printing: Amazon Kindle Direct Publishing

Made in United States
Orlando, FL
28 February 2023